SOMEONE SOMEWHERE

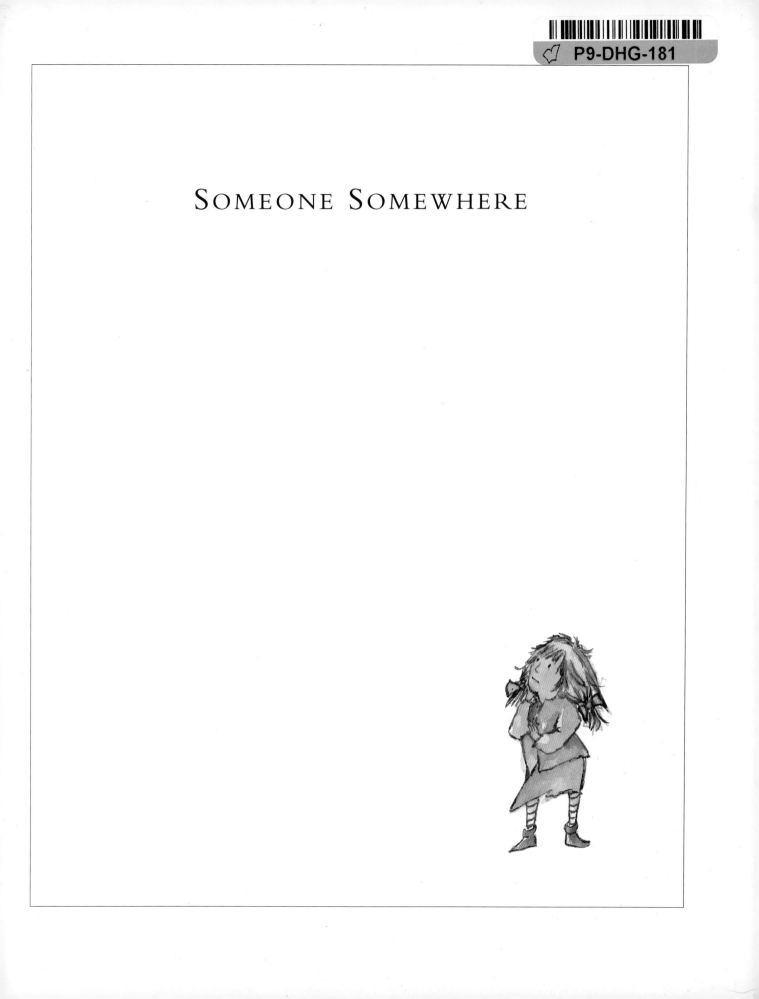

A Red Fox Book

Published by Random House Children's Books
20 Vauxhall Bridge Road, London SW1V 2SA

A division of Random House UK Ltd
London Melbourne Sydney Auckland
Johannesburg and agencies throughout the world

1 3 5 7 9 10 8 6 4 2

First published in Great Britain by The Bodley Head Children's Books 1995

Red Fox edition 1999

Printed in Singapore

RANDOM HOUSE UK Limited Reg. No. 954009

ISBN 0 091 87295 2

SOMEONE
SOMEWHERE

Henrietta Branford

Illustrated by Lesley Harker

RED FOX

To Gina Pollinger - H B

THERE was once a child who never knew her mother. Well, perhaps she did when she was very little. But time passed, she did not see her any more, and slowly she forgot her.

She was brought up by a nurse who made her wash her hands and brush her hair and eat cabbage and change her socks and go to bed at bedtime.

The nurse taught her everything she needed to know, especially all the things that she must never do. 'Promise me,' she said, 'NEVER to play in the deep, dark forest.'

'Why not?' asked the child.

'Because nobody knows what's in there,' said the nurse. And that, she thought, was that.

But it wasn't.

Time passed and the child forgot her mother's face, her
voice, the smell of her skin, and how she used to sing at
night. And the more she forgot her, the more she missed her,
until one day she could bear it no longer.

The child remembered her nurse's warning: Nobody knows what's in the forest. But then, she thought, nobody knows what isn't. Maybe all that I have lost is in there. And off she went to find out.

She came to the edge of the town and there beyond lay the deep, dark forest. And in she went, and on she went, and the trees grew thick about her, and she began to feel afraid.

Wouldn't you?

'Hello?' called the child. 'Is anybody there?'
Nobody seemed to be, and she walked on.

Presently she met an old woman.

'What are you doing alone in the forest?' asked the old woman.

'Looking for something,' said the child.

'What are you looking for?' asked the old woman.

The child shook her head. She couldn't remember what she was looking for. She only knew that it was something nice, and she wanted it.

'Never mind,' said the old woman. 'I want a child to fetch my firewood and trim my toenails and catch my cat and dish up my dinner. You'll do.'

'No I won't!' said the child, and she ran off under the trees.

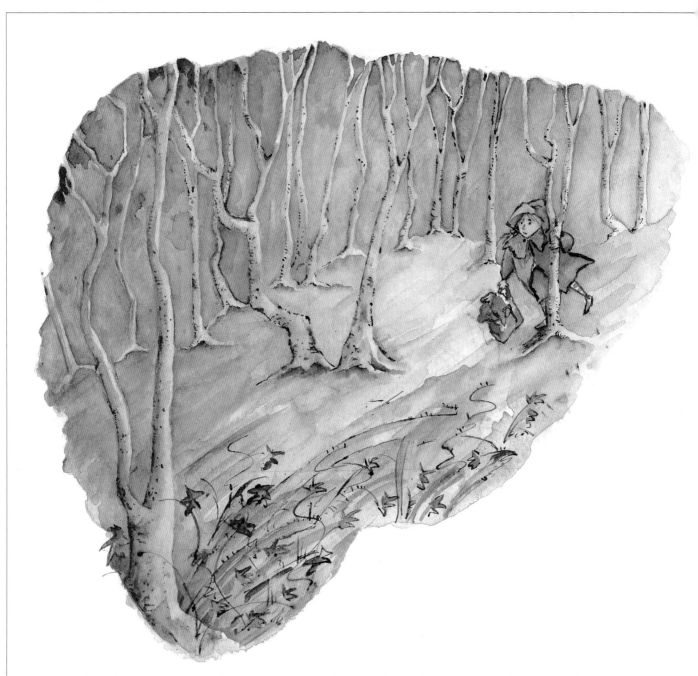

Night began to fall, creepy and spooky, the way it does in the forest, and the child began to think about witches and wolves. 'I wish I had stayed with my nurse,' she said. But deep in her heart she was glad that she hadn't. So she climbed a tree, wrapped herself in her blanket, and went to sleep.

In the morning things looked better, and she went on her way.

She came to a little hut in a clearing and outside on a rickety bench there sat a woodman.

'What are you doing alone in the forest?' asked the woodman.

'Looking for something,' said the child.

'What are you looking for?' asked the woodman.

The child shook her head. She couldn't remember what she was looking for. She only knew that it was something nice, and she wanted it.

'Don't go,' said the woodman. 'Stay here with me.'

'No!' said the child. 'I would rather be lonely on my own until I find what I am looking for.'

On she went, until she came to a dark river winding through the forest. The river turned around a pile of rocks and spread itself into a deep, still pool. A boat bobbed on the water and a woman waved at her.

'Come over,' she called. 'Come to lunch!'

'Thank you, I will,' called the child, and she climbed into a rowing boat.

'We're sailing on down river after lunch,' the woman said. 'Will you give up your search and come with us?'

'No,' said the child, 'I cannot.'

Night fell, and with it fell the first snow of winter.

Snow's early, thought the child. I must find shelter for tonight.

She looked around, and off in the distance she saw a most peculiar sight. A big old hollow log lay on its side, half buried in glistening snow. From out of each end of the hollow log blew plumes of steam. As she drew nearer to the log the child heard a deep rumbling grumble which came and went with the plumes of steam.

'Thank goodness I brought my torch,' she said to herself, and she bent down and shone a beam of yellow light into the hollow log. Inside the log the child saw one of the most comfortable and comforting sights she had ever seen.

There was a mother bear, and a father bear, and three cubs, all curled and cuddled and cossetted around each other in a great furry heap of steam-breathing, rumble-grumbling, sleepy-winter-hibernation-bearfulness.

'Mother!' she whispered. 'I've found you! Can I come in?'

Deep in her winter sleep, the mother bear heard the child. 'Of course you can,' she growled.

So the child crawled into the hollow log and settled herself comfortably against the big velvet stomach of the mother bear, and there she stayed all winter.

Spring came to the forest round about April. Suddenly the winter was past, flowers appeared and the birds sang from dawn till dusk.

The bears stretched, and breathed deep, and scratched six months' worth of itches.

The cubs looked out of the hollow log at the greening forest. They heard birds singing and bees buzzing and they scrambled to their feet and set off to explore the woods.

Father bear looked at mother bear. 'How about a walk in the woods?' he said.

Just then mother bear caught sight of the child, still asleep in the log.

'Wait a minute,' she said to her husband. 'There's a child in our log. I remember now. She came in last October when the snow was falling. She called me Mother.'

'She looks like breakfast to me,' said father bear.

'Don't be so unkind!' scolded mother bear. 'I'm going to wake her up.'

So father bear went off on his own feeling grumpy, and mother bear gently woke the sleeping child.

'Good morning poppet,' she said, licking the child with her warm wet tongue. 'Did you sleep well?'

'Yes, thank you Mother,' said the child. 'Once I found you I slept like a log.'

'In a log,' corrected mother bear gently. 'You slept in a log. And now it is spring. My cubs have gone off into the wide world to seek their fortunes, and I suppose you'll be wanting to do the same.'

'Will I?' asked the child.
  'I expect so,' said mother bear, with a sigh.

The child looked at herself. She had grown, but not as much as the young bears. She had found a mother. She had slept through the spring, and through the bitter winter safe on her mother's belly.

'If it's all the same to you, Mother,' she said, 'I will stay with you through the spring, and through the summer and the autumn too. I will sleep one more winter with you in the hollow log. After that, I may go off to seek my fortune. I'll see how I feel.'

Mother bear smiled a warm wide smile. 'It's better than all the same to me, my child,' she answered.

'Then I'll stay,' said the child. And she did.

Wouldn't you?